WELCOME TO THE STONE AGE . . .
AND THE WORLD OF THE CAVEMICE!

CAPITAL: OLD MOUSE CITY

POPULATION: WE'RE NOT SURE. (MATH DOESN'T EXIST YET!) BUT BESIDES CAVEMICE, THERE ARE PLENTY OF DINOSAURS, WAY TOO MANY SABER-TOOTHED TIGERS, AND FEROCIOUS CAVE BEARS — BUT NO MOUSE HAS EVER HAD THE COURAGE TO COUNT THEM!

TYPICAL FOOD: PETRIFIED CHEESE SOUP

NATIONAL HOLIDAY: GREAT ZAP DAY, WHICH CELEBRATES THE DISCOVERY OF FIRE. RODENTS EXCHANGE GRILLED CHEESE SANDWICHES ON THIS HOLIDAY.

NATIONAL DRINK: MAMMOTH MILKSHAKES

CLIMATE: Unpredictable, WITH FREQUENT METEOR SHOWERS.

cheese soup

milkshake

MONEY

SEASHELLS OF ALL SHAPES AND SIZES.

MEASUREMENT

THE MAIN UNIT OF MEASUREMENT IS BASED ON THE LENGTH OF THE TAIL OF THE LEADER OF THE VILLAGE. A UNIT CAN BE DIVIDED INTO A HALF-TAIL OR QUARTER-TAIL. THE LEADER IS ALWAYS READY TO PRESENT HIS TAIL WHEN THERE IS A DISPUTE.

THE CAVEMICE

Geronimo

Trap

Thea

Benjamin

Bugsy Wugsy

Hercule Poirat

Grandma Ratrock

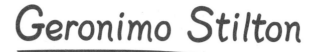

Geronimo Stilton

CAVEMICE

THE STONE
OF FIRE

Scholastic Inc.

No part of this publication may be reproduced, stored in a retrieval system, or transmitted in any form or by any means, electronic, mechanical, photocopying, recording, or otherwise, without written permission from the copyright holder. For information regarding permission, please contact: Atlantyca S.p.A., Via Leopardi 8, 20123 Milan, Italy; e-mail foreignrights@atlantyca.it, www.atlantyca.com.

ISBN 978-0-545-44774-4

Copyright © 2011 by Edizioni Piemme S.p.A., Corso Como 15, 20154 Milan, Italy.

International Rights © Atlantyca S.p.A.

English translation © 2013 by Atlantyca S.p.A.

GERONIMO STILTON names, characters, and related indicia are copyright, trademark, and exclusive license of Atlantyca S.p.A. All rights reserved. The moral right of the author has been asserted.

Based on an original idea by Elisabetta Dami.

www.geronimostilton.com

Published by Scholastic Inc., 557 Broadway, New York, NY 10012. SCHOLASTIC and associated logos are trademarks and/or registered trademarks of Scholastic Inc.

Stilton is the name of a famous English cheese. It is a registered trademark of the Stilton Cheese Makers' Association. For more information, go to www.stiltoncheese.com.

Text by Geronimo Stilton
Original title *Via le zampe dalla pietra di fuoco!*
Cover by Flavio Ferron
Illustrations by Giuseppe Facciotto (design) and Daniele Verzini (color)
Graphics by Marta Lorini

Special thanks to Tracey West
Translated by Emily Clement
Interior design by Becky James

24 23 22 21 20 19   20 21 22 23 24/0

Printed in the U.S.A.   40
First printing, January 2013

MANY AGES AGO, ON PREHISTORIC MOUSE ISLAND, THERE WAS A VILLAGE CALLED OLD MOUSE CITY. IT WAS INHABITED BY BRAVE *RODENT SAPIENS* KNOWN AS THE CAVEMICE.

DANGERS SURROUNDED THE MICE AT EVERY TURN: EARTHQUAKES, METEOR SHOWERS, FEROCIOUS DINOSAURS, AND FIERCE GANGS OF SABER-TOOTHED TIGERS. BUT THE BRAVE CAVEMICE FACED IT ALL WITH A SENSE OF HUMOR, AND WERE ALWAYS READY TO LEND A HAND TO OTHERS.

HOW DO I KNOW THIS? I DISCOVERED AN ANCIENT BOOK WRITTEN BY MY ANCESTOR, GERONIMO STILTONOOT! HE CARVED HIS STORIES INTO STONE TABLETS AND ILLUSTRATED THEM WITH HIS ETCHINGS.

I AM PROUD TO SHARE THESE STONE AGE STORIES WITH YOU. THE EXCITING ADVENTURES OF THE CAVEMICE WILL MAKE YOUR FUR STAND ON END, AND THE JOKES WILL TICKLE YOUR WHISKERS! HAPPY READING!

Geronimo Stilton

WARNING! DON'T IMITATE THE CAVEMICE. WE'RE NOT IN THE STONE AGE ANYMORE!

CLANG! CLANG!

My dear mouse friends, I hope you enjoy this story. I have spent many hours CHISELING it into STONE for you!

CLANG!
CLANG!

My ears were **ringing** from the pounding of the chisel, even though I was wearing my earmuffs.

But wait! I should introduce myself.

My name is **GERONIMO STILTONOOT**, and I'm sure that you have figured out by now that I am a cavemouse. I live in the village of Old Mouse City.

I run *The Stone Gazette*, the city's most famouse newspaper. (Actually, it's a stone slab. Paper hasn't been invented yet.) We carve one for every rodent in the city!

It's hard work, but life is hard for us **CAVEMICE**. When you live in the **STONE AGE**, danger is waiting around every corner!

We cavemice risk our **FUR** every time we step out of our caves. That's why I wrote up my *will* just this morning. You never know what might happen! For example, a

giant **meteorite** could fall from the sky and squash me. Or the volcano could explode

with **boiling lava** the color of fiery orange cheddar.

Or maybe Tiger Khan will invade with his army of saber-toothed **TIGERS**. Or a rampaging **T. REX** could chomp on my tail or bury me in a giant pile of dung. (Yuck! What a terrible way to go!)

Boiling lava!

You're tiger meat, mouse!

Not the tail!

Or worst of all — the **GREAT ZAP** could strike me down and singe my fur!

Fortunately, **disasters** like these don't happen every day. But there are plenty of other daily dangers to worry about. For example, the **MAIL-A-DACTYL** is always dropping letters carved in stone right on top of my head! *Ouch!* Sorry, what was I saying?

Oh, yes. *My will* . . .

I keep it here at the entrance to my **CAVE**, and every once in a while I make a few changes.

Phew! What a smell!

The Great Zap!

Watch your head. Special delivery!

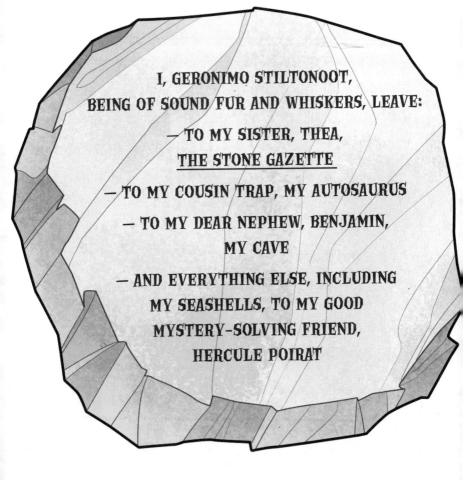

I, GERONIMO STILTONOOT,
BEING OF SOUND FUR AND WHISKERS, LEAVE:
— TO MY SISTER, THEA,
THE STONE GAZETTE
— TO MY COUSIN TRAP, MY AUTOSAURUS
— TO MY DEAR NEPHEW, BENJAMIN,
MY CAVE
— AND EVERYTHING ELSE, INCLUDING
MY SEASHELLS, TO MY GOOD
MYSTERY-SOLVING FRIEND,
HERCULE POIRAT

On the wall next to my will is a cave **PAINTING** of my family and friends. I had it painted by Pablo Picasstone, the village artist, so I could always be close to them. They are more important to me than cheese.

If it weren't for them, I'd probably be **extinct** by now!

PABLO PICASSTONE
IN FRONT OF HIS
PAINTING
Moose at Sunset

Let me introduce everyone in the painting to you. The one with **white** fur shaped like an onion on top of her head is **GRANDMA RATROCK**. She's a very strict rodent! If I spill even a crumb of cheese on my clothes, she's the first one to **SCOLD** me. She says she does it for my own good.

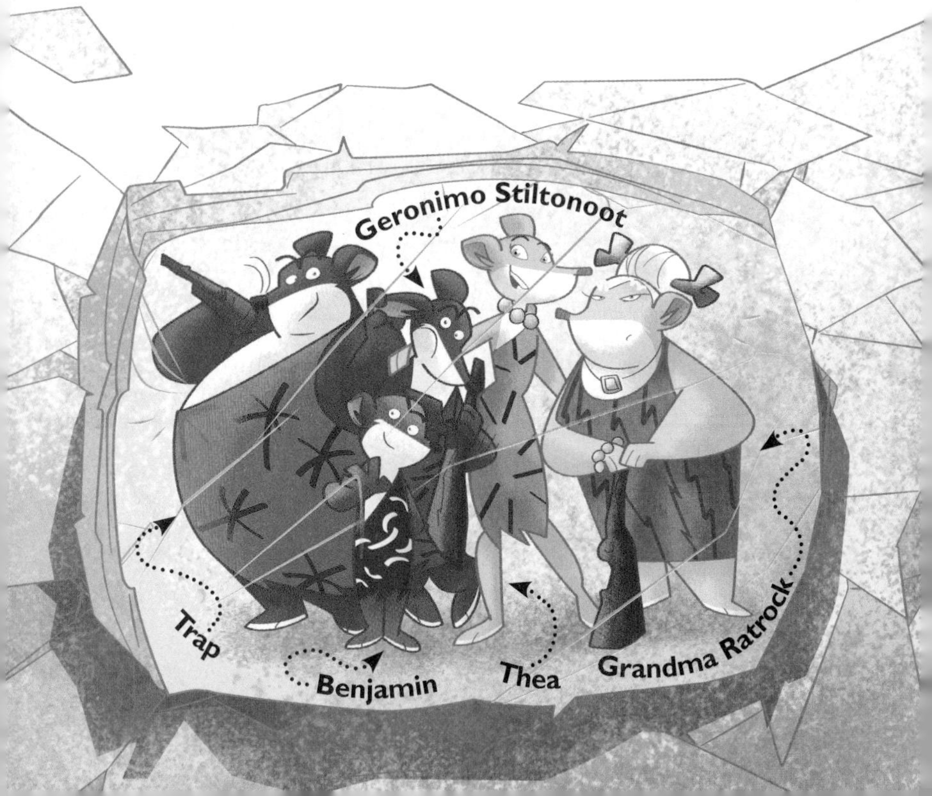

Geronimo Stiltonoot

Trap

Benjamin

Thea

Grandma Ratrock

The rodent who's pinching my right ear is my cousin **Trap**. He never misses a chance to play a **trick** on me! He runs the Rotten Tooth Tavern, which is famouse for its deep-fried cheese nuggets.

That's my sister, **THEA**, in the purple dress. She's a very lively and active rodent! She's a special reporter for *The Stone Gazette,* and she's always on the hunt for a scoop.

And that **cute** young rodent in front is my nephew, **BENJAMIN**. He's very smart — as sharp as cheddar, I always say.

Like I said, my family is very **important** to me. We are always there for one another, no matter what. That's the only way to survive in the **STONE AGE**!

A DANGEROUS MORNING, AS USUAL

That **morning** in Old Mouse City was just as dangerous as always. Every time I step outside, I'm never sure if I'll survive or become **extinct**! After checking my will again, I got ready to go out. I stuck my snout out of the **CAVE**, glancing up at the sky. There were no meteorites RAINING down on me, and the mail-a-dactyl wasn't dropping any **heavy** stones.

It looked clear, so I scampered as quickly as I could to the offices of *The Stone Gazette*. My reporters were already carving away at their tablets.

I said hello and then went into my study. Do you know what a study is? It's where you think, think, think, and then . . . you think some more!

After I thought as much as I could, I picked up my CHISEL and started to carve my story onto thick stone tablets. What a tough job!

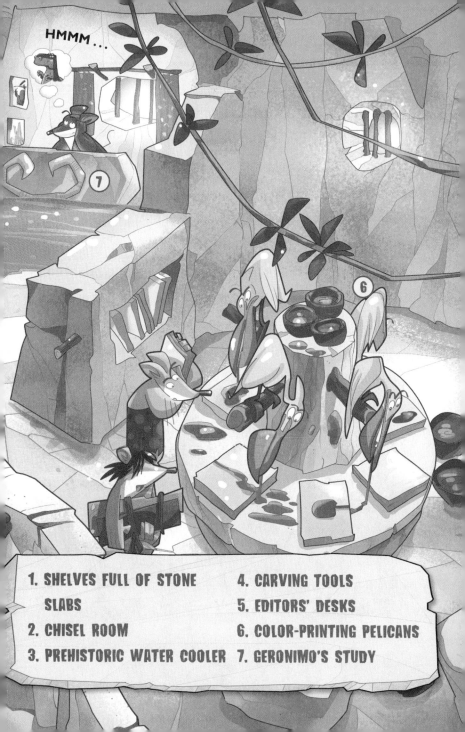

That same morning, my sister, Thea, had hopped onto the back of her autosaurus, a **VELOCIRAPTOR** named Grunty. Even though Thea has tamed him, I always try to keep far away from him. He's a carnivore, and he's always trying to BITE something. Unfortunately, sometimes it's my tail!

Thea came into my study, and Grunty bit

Grunty

MODEL: Turbo velociraptor

SIZE: About half of a T. rex's tail

AGE: Young, but with big teeth

FUEL: Small pieces of fresh meat

the cheese-filled donut I was eating right out of my paw!

"Hey!" I complained. "That was my **breakfast**! Thea, I told you to keep that biting dinosaur out of the office!"

"But he's just a little baby!" Thea said. "His teeth are just little tiny baby teeth."

She hopped off Grunty.

I'm here!

"By the way, I need to leave him with you," she said. "I have an appointment with the **fur stylist**."

As soon as Thea turned around, Grunty **BIT** my ear!

"**Ow!**" I moaned. "Baby teeth? Those are the **FANGS** of a carnivore!"

Grunty innocently *licked* Thea's paw.

"Don't be silly, Geronimo," she said. "Grunty wouldn't hurt a fly!"

She left my study before I could argue. As I rubbed my sore ear, Grunty **CHOMPED DOWN ON MY TAIL**!

I grabbed my **club** and waved it around, trying to get him to back off. "Stay where you are, you **Scaly-faced**, slimy reptile!"

Grunty just grinned and blew a raspberry. **"Pfthhhhhhhhhp!"**

Then he began jumping all over my study, roaring in his scary voice, sticking his nose into everything, and **DES+R⊙YING** the tablets I had just carved. I ran after him, trying to scare him by waving my club.

"S⊤⊙P, you overgrown tablet-breaker!"

But it didn't work. Every time I took a **SWING** with my club, Grunty nudged me off balance with his tail.

17

Overgrown lizard!

Get out of here!

So I ended up **SMASHING** my massive stone desk, destroying my statue of Grandma Ratrock, and then totally breaking my eggy bank — I **PULVERIZED** my entire emergency stash of seashells!

Finally, I stopped to catch my **BREATH**. I looked around and gasped. **OH, NO!** My study now looked like it had been hit by a meteorite!

I felt just as **destroyed** as the things in my study. All my hard work was in pieces!

I waved my club again. "Get out of here, you overgrown lizard!" I yelled. "Thea thinks you are a helpless baby, but I know the truth! You are a beast! Now **GET OUT** of here right now!"

At that moment my sister, Thea, returned. Grunty immediately knelt down and began to whimper like a **scared little mouselet**.

BONES AND STONES! What a little phony! Thea threw her arms around him.

"Shame on you, Geronimo!" she scolded me. "Treating a poor little **defenseless baby** like that!"

I tried to explain to her that the "defenseless baby" was a dangerous beast who liked to **bite** me and had tried to destroy my things, but she wouldn't listen. She has a soft spot for that creature. As they left, Grunty turned and blew one last raspberry at me.

"Pfthhhhhhhp!"

With a sigh, I sat down at my desk (or what was left of it) and tried to focus on chiseling the latest **NEWS**.

WATCH YOUR TAIL!

When I was done, I headed outside to my own **autosaurus**. Mine is a peaceful, plant-eating triceratops (and much nicer than Grunty). But I was horrified to find a **traffic ticket** on its collar!

I read the message cut into the stone:

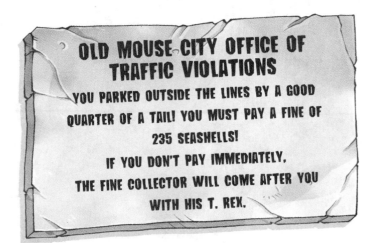

OLD MOUSE CITY OFFICE OF TRAFFIC VIOLATIONS
YOU PARKED OUTSIDE THE LINES BY A GOOD QUARTER OF A TAIL! YOU MUST PAY A FINE OF 235 SEASHELLS!
IF YOU DON'T PAY IMMEDIATELY,
THE FINE COLLECTOR WILL COME AFTER YOU WITH HIS T. REX.

At the thought of the fine collector and his ferocious T. rex, my autosaurus and I **SHIVERED**. They say if you don't pay, you could lose your tail in one bite!

BONES AND STONES, I'D REALLY LIKE TO KEEP MY TAIL!

I climbed into the saddle and scolded my autosaurus. "Why didn't you move before he gave you the ticket?"

"You're the one who told me not to move from this spot," he replied.

I **sighed**. Arguing with an autosaurus is as useless as arguing with my sister, Thea!

Gasp!

Autosaurus

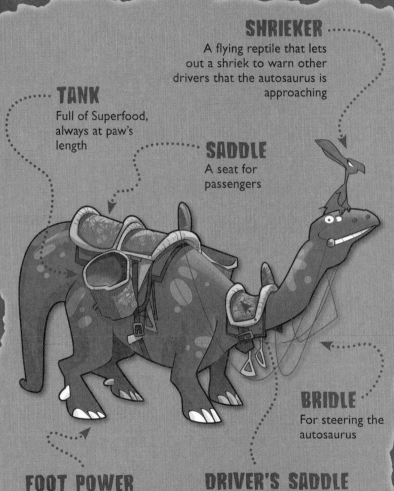

SHRIEKER
A flying reptile that lets out a shriek to warn other drivers that the autosaurus is approaching

TANK
Full of Superfood, always at paw's length

SADDLE
A seat for passengers

BRIDLE
For steering the autosaurus

FOOT POWER
Who needs a motor when you've got powerful feet?

DRIVER'S SADDLE
Where the driver sits

"Well, why don't you get moving?" I asked a little impatiently.

My autosaurus THUMPED his tail on the ground a few times, raising a cloud of dust. Then he replied, "Aren't you forgetting something important?"

BONES AND STONES, HOW CARELESS OF ME!

I had forgotten to feed him his Superfruit Smoothie that morning. (Since he's a plant eater, he gets all his energy from fruits and vegetables.) Luckily, I always keep an extra tank of it hanging from the saddle.

"Here you go!" I said, feeding him. "EAT UP! But don't move your tail, or the T. rex will fine us for disturbing the dust!"

The autosaurus devoured the smoothie in one gulp and then sped off. I barely had time to grab the bridle as he *hurried* down the busy street that crossed Old Mouse City.

Morning traffic already clogged the street. The air was noisy with the **SQUEALS** of the shriekers, *Winged* dinosaurs that perched on the head of each autosaurus. They impatiently shouted, trying to get things moving.

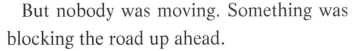

SQUEEEEAK!

SQUEEEEAK!

But nobody was moving. Something was blocking the road up ahead.

"oh, no!" I exclaimed. "Here we go again!"

It was Old Clovis, who insisted on driving a **Giant** tortoise that was slower than cheese sauce on a cold night. He **BLOCKED** up the whole road as he tried to park.

27

My shrieker squealed loudly, but it was no use! None of the noise was helping at all. But then I heard a different **NOISE** — the voice of my good friend, Hercule Poirat. *"Out of the waaaaaaay!"* he yelled at the top of his lungs.

Bam! He crashed into me from behind and I ran into an autosaurus carrying boxes of **tomatoes**. *Splat!* They fell right on top of me!

Blinded by tomato sauce, I ran into a **cheese** cart, spilling the cheese all over. My autosaurus stumbled and we knocked into a **BREAD** cart. The loaves went *FLYING*!

I was covered in sauce, cheese, and bread. When I wiped off the **MUSHY** mess, I saw Hercule taking a bite of the mix.

Then he smiled. "Hey!" he cried. "You just invented **prehistoric pizza**!"

As soon as Hercule said it, the ears of a nearby rodent began to twitch. I knew he was one of the spies working for **SALLY ROCKMOUSEN**, host of Old Mouse City's Gossip Radio show.

Whenever there's **gossip**, Sally stands outside her cave, which is high on a hill. She **SHOUTS** the news all over the village!

Thanks to her spies, Sally always knows whenever anything interesting happens. When one of her rodents hears something, they **squeal** to another spy, who squeals to another spy, who squeals to another . . . well, you get the idea!

The problem with this is that by the time the **NEWS** gets to Sally, it ends up completely **different** than when it started! So I was trying to get away from the **RADIO SPY** when I felt a claw tapping me on my shoulder. I turned and saw the threatening face of a **T. REX** at the end of a traffic officer's leash!

"You've made quite a mess," snarled the officer. "Will you take a fine, or a **BITE**?"

Geronimo has invented prehistoric pizza!

...prehistoric peas!

"I'll pay, I'll pay!" I said, terrified.

Geronimo Stiltonoot has a prehistoric pimple!

...prehistoric people!

SPECIAL DELIVERY FOR GERONIMO!

"Pay up, Geronimo!" Hercule urged me.

I eyed the T. rex's **FANGS** and quickly turned over my shells.

When the traffic officer left, Hercule went back to his autosaurus.

"What a **LUCKY** coincidence it is to run into you today!" he said cheerfully. "I've been meaning to ask you something. . . ."

"**Lucky?** You call that lucky?" I interrupted him. "I'm a **MESS**! And what a waste of perfectly good cheese!"

Hercule snorted. "Don't be cranky. We have more *important* things to deal with! I need you to come with me. There's a problem at the *Old Mouse City Mouseum*. This morning . . ."

Just then, I heard the whirring of wings above us. It was followed by a whistle, and then a sharp squeal.

IT WAS A MAIL-A-DACTYL!

Everyone ran for cover. But I slipped on some tomato sauce and fell!

The mail-a-dactyl squealed,

"MAIL! MAAAAAIL! MAAAAAAIL!"

A big stone tablet that would have knocked out a **MAMMOTH** fell on my head. There was a message written on it:

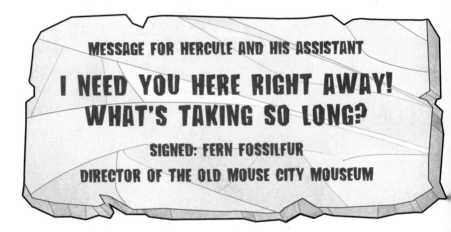

MESSAGE FOR HERCULE AND HIS ASSISTANT

I NEED YOU HERE RIGHT AWAY! WHAT'S TAKING SO LONG?

SIGNED: FERN FOSSILFUR
DIRECTOR OF THE OLD MOUSE CITY MOUSEUM

As I read, a **BUMP** the size of an extra-large cheese nugget popped up on top of my head.

"**HURRY**, let's go!" Hercule said, grabbing my paw. "We don't want her to send another message."

"But how will we get there?" I asked. "The traffic is still backed up."

Hercule grinned. "The **Subwaysaurus**, of course!"

I gulped. I hate riding the Subwaysaurus. But I didn't have a choice. I didn't want to risk getting another **BUMP** on the head!

So we headed down to the Metrocave. We paid our admission — a slice of meat to the **TICKET-O-SAURUS**, who let us through the turnstile. Then we waited for the arrival of the enormouse **WORM** that would take us to the mouseum. That's right — a worm!

Chomp!
Chomp!
Chomp!

Subwaysaurus

An enormouse prehistoric worm that moves along an underground
riverbed. The inhabitants of Old Mouse City use it to quickly get
from one part of the city to another. At each station, a conductor
stops the Subwaysaurus by putting a banana leaf in front of its
eyes. Then he gently tickles the creature, and when it opens its
mouth to laugh, the passengers hop inside. At the next station,
the same process is repeated, and the rodents get off.

When the Subwaysaurus slid into the station, the **conductor** stopped it with a huge fan made of **banana** leaves. He tickled it, and the Subwaysaurus opened its mouth to laugh.

"Let them off!" the conductor shouted as the passengers got out.

Then he tickled the Subwaysaurus again. "PASSENGERS INTO THE BELLY!" he shouted.

You look pretty green. Are you feeling Subwaysaurus sick?

As I climbed aboard, I barely got my tail out of the way before the giant worm closed its enormouse mouth. Then it started to sway **back** and *forth*, back and forth, back and forth. My stomach started to go **back** and *forth*, back and forth, back and forth.

I felt **Subwaysaurus sick**!

GLUUUUURB!

Finally, we arrived at the mouseum stop. My poor tummy felt like it was filled with curdled cheese. I climbed up the steps and joined Hercule by the mouseum entrance. **Fern Fossilfur**, the mouseum director, was impatiently waiting for us.

DID YOU GET THAT, GERONIMO?

Fern was a tall, thin rodent with a nose as **POINTY** as the horn of a triceratops.

She stared at the **BUMP** on my head and said, "Oh, good, I see that you got my message! There's no time to waste. I'll show you the scene of the crime. Someone stole our most precious artifact: the **STONE OF FIRE**!"

Then she looked at me more closely, her eyes narrowing. "Aren't you Geronimo Stiltonoot, the famouse editor of *The Stone Gazette*? You **look** just like him."

I was about to respond, but Hercule jumped in. "Oh, he's *just* my assistant."

Fern walked away before I could protest. Hercule **whispered** to me, "Come on, Geronimo, take notes!"

Have I told you that Hercule likes all the **attention** for himself? But he's my friend, and I wanted to help. As Fern led us to the room where the **theft** took place, I took out my pocket stone tablet and chisel.

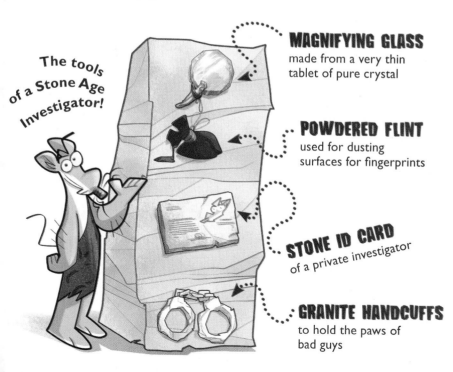

The tools of a Stone Age Investigator!

MAGNIFYING GLASS
made from a very thin tablet of pure crystal

POWDERED FLINT
used for dusting surfaces for fingerprints

STONE ID CARD
of a private investigator

GRANITE HANDCUFFS
to hold the paws of bad guys

Hercule looked very pleased with himself as he began examining the room for clues.

"Hmm, strange. There's **stalactite dust** on the ground. Chisel that down, Geronimo," he said.

"Yes, yes, I'm chiseling," I replied.

"Hmm, strange. There are **pawprints** leading to the window," he said. "Did you get that, Geronimo?"

I felt **RUSHED**. "Give me a minute! I'm chiseling as fast as my paws can go!"

"Hmm, very strange. Beneath this window, outside, I see some broken **STONES**. Did you get that, Geronimo?"

I was chiseling so fast that **STONE CHIPS** were flying everywhere, but I still couldn't keep up. "What do you think I am, a typewriter?" I snapped. "Those haven't even been invented yet!"

1. Map of the flat world (They didn't know the world was round yet!)
2. An early club
3. First wheel
4. Fossilized ham
5. Cave painting
6. Stone of Fire (missing!)
7. Scarysaurus skeleton
8. Sea dinosaur
9. Skeleton of the first cavemouse
10. Modern sculpture (or at least it was modern back then!)

Chisel, Geronimo, chisel!

Old Mouse City Mouseum

Hercule shrugged and looked at Fern. "Assistants! They're such lazy cheeseheads. Always complaining."

"I am *not* your —" I started to protest, but I was distracted by something dripping on my snout. Drip! Drip! Drip!

What could it be?

All I knew was that it had an awful SMELL!

Huff ... puff ... I'm chiseling!

I looked up at the ceiling and saw what looked like a round **hole** covered with sticky yellowish glop.

I *pointed* at it. "What's that? If you ask me, the thieves must have come in through there!"

Hercule shushed me. "Silence, assistant! Leave the talking to me!"

He walked up to Fern and pointed at the hole. Then he **repeated** my exact words!

"If you ask me, the thieves must have come in through there!"

"What is that **sticky glop**?" I asked.

He stuck his paw in the stuff and smiled triumphantly.

What's that?

"It's elementary, my dear mouse! This is fresh **dino cement**, a sticky mixture of clay, pterodactyl guano, and gum-tree resin!" I shuddered. WHAT A NASTY MESS!

Help!

Hercule leaned toward me and examined the drops on my snout.

"Aha!" he exclaimed. "Just as I expected! There are FLIES stuck in the dino cement. And this species of fly only lives in *Stinky Swamp!*"

My mind was spinning like a wheel of cheese rolling downhill. I was confused, but Hercule was confident. He led me to the roof, where he found some large pawprints left by felines!

"It's so obvious!" he boasted. "They **dropped** down from the roof, took the Stone of Fire, sealed the hole with fresh dino cement, and **fled** through the window. Did you get that, Geronimo?"

It's elementary, my dear mouse!

THE ROTTEN TOOTH TAVERN

Hercule explained all the **CLUES** to me again, but I still felt like I was looking at the case through a **block** of cheese.

"So who stole the **STONE OF FIRE**?" I asked, perplexed.

He rolled his eyes. "You still don't understand? Your head must be made of granite! The **STONE OF FIRE** was stolen by a feline. A cat! This feline had to be very clever and stealthy to break into the mouseum without getting caught. And the thief only wanted the stone, because nothing else in the mouseum was taken."

"What **feline** would want the Stone of

Fire?" asked Fern.

"That is still a **MYSTERY**," Hercule replied. "But we'll soon solve it, I promise!"

He began to stroke his whiskers. "Hmm. We need more information. And a good place for that is the Rotten Tooth Tavern! It's run by an annoying mouse who never stops talking. His chatter makes my skull **rattle**!"

"Well, actually . . ." I began.

"That rodent is **obnoxious**!" Hercule interrupted. "You're lucky you don't know him!"

I sighed. "Actually, I *do* know him. In fact, I'm related to him. That rodent is my cousin **Trap**!"

"Oh! Well, maybe you can tell him to keep his **trap** shut sometimes," Hercule suggested.

"I don't think that's possible," I said, shaking my head.

We said good-bye to Fern and walked to Trap's tavern by the *SEA*. Inside, we saw a line of rodents waiting to get up onstage. The cavemouse onstage told a **joke**, and the audience laughed. But his next joke wasn't as funny, and they all began to pelt him with **ROTTEN EGGS**!

Of course! It was the **ANNUAL CAVEMOUSE**

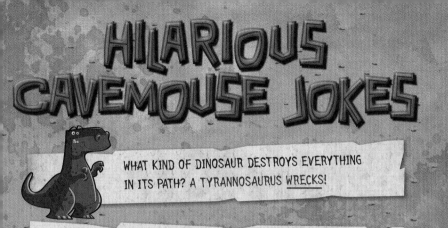

HILARIOUS CAVEMOUSE JOKES

WHAT KIND OF DINOSAUR DESTROYS EVERYTHING IN ITS PATH? A TYRANNOSAURUS <u>WRECKS</u>!

AT A RESTAURANT, A CAVEMOUSE COMPLAINED TO THE WAITER, "THERE'S A FLY IN MY SOUP! BRING ME ANOTHER ONE!" THE WAITER WENT BACK TO THE KITCHEN AND SAID, "CHEF! ANOTHER FLY FOR THE CUSTOMER!"

WHAT KIND OF MUSIC DOES A CAVEMOUSE LIKE BEST? <u>ROCK</u> MUSIC!

TWO SABER-TOOTHED TIGERS WERE WALKING IN THE DESERT. ONE TIGER TURNED TO THE OTHER AND SAID, "I HAVE GOOD NEWS AND BAD NEWS. WHICH DO YOU WANT FIRST?"
"THE BAD NEWS," HIS FRIEND REPLIED.
"WE'LL HAVE NOTHING BUT SAND TO EAT TODAY."
"SO WHAT'S THE GOOD NEWS?" ASKED HIS FRIEND.
"LOOK HOW MUCH THERE IS!"

WHAT KIND OF SANDWICH DOES A CAVEMOUSE LIKE BEST? A <u>CLUB</u> SANDWICH!

JOKE CHAMPIONSHIP! How could I have forgotten? Every year, mice competed to win the big prize: a super deluxe autosaurus with turbo-charged feet.

We **DODGED** the rotten eggs flying around the room and went looking for Trap. My cousin approached us with his business partner, **Greasella Stonyfur**. She's the head chef at the tavern, and she's famouse in Old Mouse City for the greasy dishes she makes. It takes a whole **GEOLOGICAL ERA** to digest her prehistoric fried cheese nuggets!

Greasella Stonyfur

Trap

54

A CAVEMOUSE RECIPE

MEATBALLS IN PRIMORDIAL SOUP

By Greasella Stonyfur

(Remember, always ask an adult for help in the kitchen!)

INGREDIENTS FOR 4 SERVINGS:

6 cups of broth
1 pound of ground beef
¼ cup chopped parsley
1 egg

¼ cup grated Parmesan cheese
1 slice of bread
milk
salt and pepper, about ½ tsp each

Soak the piece of bread in some milk and then squeeze out the excess liquid. Mix the meat with the egg, parsley, cheese, soaked bread, and salt and pepper. Mix it thoroughly, adding some bread crumbs if it's too wet. Form into small balls. Bring the broth to a boil and gently drop in the meatballs. Cook for 15 minutes or until meatballs are no longer pink inside. Serve hot, in broth, with more grated cheese.

BON APPÉTIT!

Greasella held out a dish **dripping** with sauce. "Would you like some Gorgonzola fondue?"

"No, thank you," I said quickly. "We're just here to get some information."

Trap pointed to a **SUSPICIOUS**-looking mouse sitting in the corner. "Then you need to talk to Carl Crookedtail. He always knows everything that happens in *Old Mouse City*. He should be able to help you."

We walked up to Carl's table and introduced ourselves.

"The **STONE OF FIRE** has been stolen," Hercule said. "We think the **THIEF** is a feline, but we don't know who it is."

Carl looked around to make sure nobody was **LISTENING**. Then he motioned for us to get closer. I felt excited. Did he know the thief?

"Based on what you've told me," he said, "I can tell you that the thief is a **feline**!"

"We just told you that!" I said, frustrated.

"Thanks for nothing!"

FLIGHT TO BUGVILLE!

Greasella overheard us. "Forget him — I can help you!" she said. "I heard from my cousin that **TIGER KHAN** has a big invention collection. My cousin heard it from his **dentist**, who heard it from his **aunt**, who heard it from a **PRISONER** who was held by **TIGER KHAN** and managed to escape!"

I **shivered**. Everyone knows Tiger Khan. He's the terrifying chief of the **SABER-TOOTHED SQUAD**, a ferocious tribe of saber-toothed tigers from Bugville. He's the number one enemy of Old Mouse City!

"I want to go **HOME**," I moaned to Hercule. "I'm not really your assistant!"

Hercule shook his head. "You may not be my assistant, but you're my **friend**, right? I know you wouldn't let me face the Saber-Toothed Squad all by myself!"

Hercule had me there. We cavemice prize *friendship* above all else. I agreed to go with him, and Hercule and I hurried to the Old Mouse City flightport. He walked up to the counter, bought **TWO REALLY CHEAP TICKETS**, and proudly ran back to me.

Here are our two cheapest tickets!

Thank you!

59

"I got a great deal, Geronimo!" he said. "I found two tickets at a deep **DISCOUNT**!"

But when I saw the flying dinosaur waiting for us on the runway, I knew why the price was so low. It was an ancient, worn-out balloonosaurus. Its big belly was filled with AIR, and it FLOATED about ten feet off the ground. Ropes tied it to stakes plunged into the ground, and a ragged wicker basket hung beneath it.

I gulped. "Are you sure this balloonosaurus can make such a long journey?"

"No big deal!" said the pilot confidently. "Climb on board. It's almost time for TAKEOFF!"

When I got on board, the pilot handed me a piece of fur with a string attached to it and told me to strap it on. It looked like . . . a PARACHUTE.

THE BALLOONOSAURUS

Before each takeoff, the balloonosaurus is fed with a Superbean Concentrate. Its belly fills with air, causing it to float. There's always a reserve supply of Superbean Concentrate on board, in case the balloonosaurus starts to deflate.

WINGS
to help with takeoff

SUPERBEAN CAULDRON
always on hand for refills

STEERING WHEEL
to change direction

I **gulped** again. "Are you *sure* this balloonosaurus is safe?" I asked Hercule.

But then someone shouted, "Flight to Bugville!" The pilot untied the ropes and the large animal began to rise into the air, flapping its wings and **wobbling** dangerously.

I spent the whole flight **trembling** like a bowl of cheese custard, but Hercule fell sound asleep. He didn't wake up until hours later, when a **ROTTEN SMELL** hit us. He opened his eyes, sniffed the air, and announced, "We have arrived in Bugville!"

I leaned out and saw a **DARK** peninsula jutting into the water. A **buzzing** cloud covered the land.

What is that? I was wondering, when Hercule suddenly **KICKED** me from behind! I tumbled overboard as he yelled, "Pull the corrrrrrrd!"

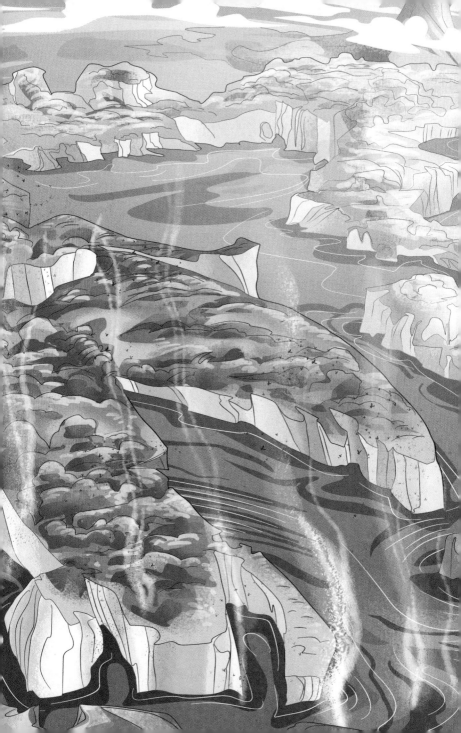

I pulled the cord, the fur opened, and I began to *swing* in the wind as the parachute carried me safely to the ground.

But then Hercule yelled, "WATCH OUT FOR THE **POOP**, STILTONOOT!"

I looked down with horror and saw enormouse **brown** piles below me, getting closer and closer. But I couldn't steer! **Squish!** I landed in a stinky mountain of dino droppings.

Blech!

ROOOOOAAAR!

I held my nose and tried to climb out of the pile, when suddenly I felt the ground **shake**. I looked up and saw an enormouse **TAIL** raised above me!

I opened my mouth to *SCREAM*, but Hercule slapped a paw over my snout.

"Quiet, Geronimo!" he warned. "That **T. REX** is going in the same direction we are. Let's hitch a ride. Just don't let it see you grab on to its tail — it might get **ANGRY**."

"Or it might **eat us**!" I added. "Don't worry. I'll be as quiet as a mouse!"

We grabbed on to the **GIANT TAIL** as the T. rex stomped across the ground.

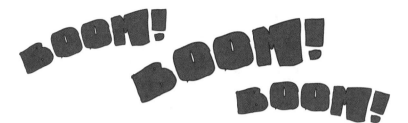

I hung on as tightly
as I could. What a
wild ride!

Luckily, it didn't
take long to get
to **TIGER
KHAN'S** camp.

"Here we are,
Geronimo!"
Hercule announced.
"The camp of the
Saber-Toothed
Squad!"

We let go of the
tail and landed with

Ack!

a **thud** on the rocky ground. Then we quickly **HID** behind a boulder and watched the scene below. The camp was crawling with saber-toothed tigers with **LONG FANGS** and sharp claws.

EEEK! I HAVE A FEAR OF FELINES!

"Um, Hercule, what's your plan?" I whispered.

"Plan? What **PLAN**?" my friend replied.

"What?" I cried. "You mean you brought me all the way here without having a **PLAN**?"

Hercule shrugged. "I thought we could **MAKE IT UP** as we go," he said calmly.

"Make it up?" I asked, almost **shouting**. "What are we supposed to do?"

"Ssssh! Quiet! Do you want them to find us?" Hercule asked, putting his paw over my

MAP OF TIGER KHAN'S CAMP

1. Chief's tent
2. Chief's breakfast tent
3. Chief's weapons tent
4. Chief's treasure tent
5. Chief's personal gym
6. Fighting arena
7. Army's gym
8. Target practice
9. Generals' tents
10. Officers' tents
11. Recruits' tents
12. Storage for supply of smelly prehistoric fish
13. Prisons
14. Giant litter box
15. Stone scratching post

snout. "Okay, here's a **PLAN**. How about you creep into the Chief's tent, steal the **STONE OF FIRE**, and then . . . *scram*!"

Before I could argue, he **SHOVED** me forward.

"Hercule! This is not a good plan!" I hissed.

He ignored me. "**GO ON, Stiltonoot!** You can do it! You're smoother than cheese sauce, faster than a meteorite, more powerful than the jaws of a **T. REX**!"

I sighed and ran into the camp, hoping the **FEROCIOUS** felines wouldn't see me. My teeth chattered with fear, and cold **sweat** dripped from my whiskers. I'm not sure if I've mentioned it, but I am a complete **scaredy-mouse**!

Most of the soldiers were inside their tents, purring. **Prrrrrrrrrr!** And there was an awful **STINK** in the place — probably from

all the **ROTTING FISH** they loved to eat. I held my nose and kept running.

What a **STENCH**! It was worse than the smell of **MOLDY** mozzarella on a stale prehistoric cracker!

Suddenly, I felt something **sharp** grab my tail!

"Let me go!" I pleaded. "I'm as **TOUGH** as a cheese rind! I taste terrible!"

I turned, sure that I would find the enormouse jaws of a **TIGER** ready to devour me, but my tail was only caught on a **THORNY** bush!

I sighed with relief. I didn't need to be afraid. I'm such a **scaredy-mouse**!

I started to creep toward the largest tent in the camp, the Chief's tent. Then a dark **SHADOW** came over me, and a terrifying roar filled the air.

ROOOOOAARRRRRRR!

It wasn't a bush this time! Two **SUPER-SHARP** claws lifted me up. Terrifying **JAWS** full of long, pointy **TEETH** opened wide to bite me. The end was near, I was sure.

YUM...
RAW RODENT!

"Hey, you!" *hissed* the feline, blowing his awful breath in my face. "Consider yourself already extinct! The great **TIGER KHAN** doesn't allow intruders."

I was so **frozen** with fear that I couldn't

Roooaar!

say anything. The tiger took a closer look at me. His expression changed when he noticed my **ears** and **tail**.

"In your case, I think he'll make an **exception**," he said

with a wicked grin. "**TIGER KHAN** loves rodents. Especially raw ones!"

Panic set in. "I-I'm n-not t-tasty!" I stuttered. "I'm w-way too thin. I'm not a **meal** worthy of your great chief!"

"Don't even try to escape!"

he warned. "I'll make sure you're the perfect snack, mouse!"

Then he tossed me into a CAGE that hung from a pole and locked me in.

Let's eat him!

"You won't be getting out of here until you're nice and FAT!" he said with a sneer.

Helpless, I looked around for Hercule. Where was he **hiding**? I looked down and saw a line of **hungry** felines watching me. They licked their whiskers as **DROOL** dripped from their super-sharp fangs.

Yum!

80

"Why don't we **eat** him now?" one tiger asked.

"Yeah, he looks FAT enough!" said another.

I tried to suck in my stomach. The tiger who had caught me chased them off with a swipe of his CLAWS.

"Scram!" he roared. "This mouse isn't for you to eat. He's a tasty treat reserved for the banquet in honor of our great chief, TIGER KHAN!"

Then he pushed a big hunk of meat into the cage. "Eat up and get fat!" he commanded.

"Don't you have any CHEESE?" I asked. "Or some cheese sauce, at least?"

"Be quiet and eat up!" he yelled.

When he left, I tossed the meat into the bushes. The next morning, the TIGER returned and frowned.

"You're still not fat!" he complained.

"Bring more meat!" he yelled to the **TIGER** army. "More **FOOD** for the prisoner, right away!"

"And some cheese sauce," I whispered.

"And some **cheese sauce**!" the tiger bellowed.

"Oh, and some salt," I said.

"And some salt," he added, glaring at me.

They brought me:

6 RACKS of ribs!

15 BRONTOSAURUS eggs!

37 PTERODACTYL wings!

82 DINO drumsticks!

I covered everything with

cheese sauce and salt, and

ate until I couldn't eat another bite.

Burp!

SHAM, THE STRANGE SHAMAN

Another day passed, and I was so **FAT** I could barely fit in the cage. I knew the tigers were going to **EAT ME** very soon!

I was right. The tiger who had caught me showed up that morning.

"Tonight you will be served as a **SPECIAL treat** for Tiger Khan," he announced.

I turned as **PALE** as mozzarella. "But wh-why tonight?" I stuttered. "Let's wait a few more days. I'll be much more **DELICIOUS** if I eat some more."

The tiger shook his head. "It's been decided! Tonight there will be a huge banquet in Tiger Khan's honor. We are celebrating the **BIG**

iNVaSiON that's happening tomorrow."

"Invasion? Where?" I asked.

The tiger grinned. "*Old Mouse City,* of course!"

That's when I noticed the army of felines and **WILD BEASTS** that had gathered in the camp. They were all there to join forces with Tiger Khan! My village was **DOOMED**!

We've come from far away to conquer and destroy!

Tiger Khan had always **threatened** to attack, but we never thought he would do it. This was bad — **VERY BAD**.

One by one the soldiers arrived, and the tigers gave them **WEAPONS**, armor, and **BANNERS**.

I watched everything unfold from my cage. When the sun set, four cave bears stomped

Here comes the great . . .

. . . Tiger Khan!

into the main camp, carrying a litter that held the **BiGGEST** saber-toothed tiger of all. He had bushy whiskers and shiny fur. When he grinned his evil grin, I could see sharp **TEETH** as white as snow and as **pointy** as spears.

It was **TIGER KHAN**! I could see why everyone was so terrified of him. But what interested me most was the object he held in his right paw:

THE STONE OF FIRE!

The rumor was true. He had stolen it!

Tiger Khan climbed into his large throne and placed the stone on

a granite PEDESTAL next to him. Then he addressed his soldiers.

"My brave fighters, my SABER-TOOTHED SQUAD, and all my wild warriors, I have great news," he announced in a booming voice. "There is a new precious treasure in my collection of inventions: the powerful STONE OF FIRE!"

A murmur of SURPRISE spread through the crowd.

"I am still learning about its mysterious powers," he continued. "But I am certain that it will make us invincible. Tomorrow at dawn we will attack OLD MOUSE CITY! Now, let's begin the banquet. I'm as hungry as a lion!"

The crowd roared.

"LONG LIVE TIGER KHAN!"

89

The warriors all raised their bone clubs and waved them triumphantly.

The soldiers began to toast their leader.

"Long life and fresh meat for Tiger Khan!"

"MAY THE GREAT ZAP SAVE TIGER KHAN!"

"ENJOY YOUR FEAST, TIGER KHAN!"

I gulped as the terrifying tiger chief pointed a **SHARP CLAW** at me. "Bring me that mouse! I will eat it as an appetizer!"

Two **felines** pulled me out of the cage and dragged me to the **THRONE**. This was the end for sure!

I was about to close my eyes when I saw a very

strange visitor enter the circle. He was surrounded by a cloud of **flies**, so it was hard to see his face. He wore a **necklace** of teeth around his neck, and bracelets made of shells on his wrists and ankles. Every time he took a step, he *JANGLED*.

"Make way! Make way!" he shouted, marching slowly and solemnly. "Make way for **SHAM THE SHAMAN**!"

Even felines know that shamans have mysterious magical powers. They let him pass, murmuring,

"What a strange shaman!"

THIS MOUSE IS TABOO!

The shaman waved a long, wobbly stick topped with a tortoise **SHELL**.

"Make way for Sham the Shaman!" he yelled. "If you don't, I will transform you all into triceratops **DUNG**!"

The crowd parted. There are many shamans here in the Stone Age, and we all know not to mess with them. Their **MYSTERIOUS** powers can cause lots of trouble!

The strange shaman walked up to me and turned to the crowd.

"I have good news and **BAD NEWS**. Which would you like to hear first?" he asked.

Everyone began to argue.

"**BAD** news first!"

"No, **good** news first!"

"Fine, I'll start with the bad news," the shaman snapped. He turned to Tiger Khan. "This mouse is taboo! If you eat him, it will bring you misfortune. First, your whiskers will fall out!"

"NOOO! NOT HIS WHISKERS!" everyone shouted.

"And then your tail will lose its fur."

"Nooo! Not his tail!" everyone squealed.

Sham nodded. "And then you'll come down with measles, a cold, and a terrible stomachache. And that's not all. If you eat this mouse, you will call forth the

!"

93

This news made everyone panic.

"NOOO! NOT THE GREAT ZAP!"

"We'll be roasted! We'll be toasted!"

Even though all of his soldiers were worried, **TIGER KHAN** remained calm. He drummed his paws on the arms of his throne and **GROWLED**, "I'm not afraid of anyone or anything — not even the Great Zap! I am going to eat this mouse, and I'll eat him **RAW**! How **dare** you tell the great Khan what he can and cannot eat?"

"Be careful, Tiger Khan," the shaman warned. "Not even you can risk the wrath of the **GREAT ZAP**."

"Then show me your power, shaman!" Tiger Khan commanded with a **FIERY** look.

The shaman bowed. "As you wish," he said. "Now for the good news. I know the

94

mysterious power of the **STONE OF FIRE**, and I will explain it to you!"

Tiger Khan looked interested. "Good, good! Show me the power of this legendary stone, you **STRANGE SHAMAN**, and *maybe* I won't cut off your tail!"

The shaman looked very serious as he took the Stone of Fire from the pedestal and placed it on a **CRAGGY ROCK**. He sprinkled **dried grass** on the rock and then struck the Stone of Fire against a piece of the rock. Small **sparks** flew up and landed on the dried grass. Soon a bright **FLAME** began to burn.

"OOOOOOOOOOOh!"

The felines were amazed!

The **SHAMAN** snuck a look at me and winked. *Why would he do that?* I wondered. Then he put the **STONE OF FIRE** back on the pedestal.

"That's not all!" he shouted. "Now I will

The "Magic" of Fire

In the prehistoric era, fire was often made with two stones: a gray rock called flint and another stone containing iron. When the two stones are struck together, they produce sparks. Those sparks then ignite nearby fuel, such as dried grass or moss, to create a fire.

So the Stone of Fire isn't magic — it's just flint!

show you more of my powerful magic."

He rummaged in his bag, took out a handful of powder, and threw it on the fire. "**STRANGE MAGIC NUMBER ONE**: the Multicolored Flame!"

A strange *green* flame burst from the fire, and everyone coughed.

Strange Magic Number One!

"And now it's time for **STRANGE MAGIC NUMBER TWO**: the Disappearing Stone!" the shaman announced dramatically. He approached the pedestal and covered the Stone of Fire with a large **handkerchief**. Then he began to dance around.

Strange Magic Number Two!

"One . . . two . . . three," he chanted. Then he stopped. "Behold the power of the **GREAT ZAP**!"

He lifted the handkerchief — and the pedestal was **EMPTY**!

Tiger Khan angrily sprang toward the shaman, but Sham quickly threw another handful of grass on the fire.

"And now for **STRANGE MAGIC NUMBER THREE**: the Vanishing Mouse Appetizer!"

A thick cloud exploded from the fire, creating a dense **FOG** that spread all over the circle.

"I can't see!" Tiger Khan roared.

I couldn't see, either. But I felt someone **grab** my paw and drag me away!

THE BATTLE BEGINS

As the smoke cleared, I was relieved to see **SHAM THE SHAMAN** holding my paw.

"Sorry I took so long to save you, my friend," he whispered in my ear. That's when I realized: Sham the Shaman was **Hercule** in disguise!

Hercule

Fake tiger-skin wig

Leaf headdress

Fake tiger teeth

SHAM, THE STRANGE SHAMAN

"It wasn't easy getting together my costume," he explained. "And I had to find **SULFUR** for the special effects with the flames."

I gave him a hug. "Thank you for saving me! You're a **true friend**!"

Hercule patted my shoulder. "No time to be mushy. We have to escape before they **catch** us!"

I didn't argue. The **SABER-TOOTHED SQUAD** was right on our tails as we **raced** away from the camp as **FAST** as we could. We went so fast that by the time we reached Old Mouse City, I was **thin** again!

When we got to the city gates, we **BANGED** on them with our paws. "Open up! We're being followed by felines!" I yelled.

The gates opened and we hurried in just in time. As soon as we closed them, the tigers

arrived, scratching at the wood with their claws. Then they spread out all along the **walls** of the city, ready to attack. The city sounded an alarm.

Hercule and I sped to the mouseum, where we safely restored the **STONE OF FIRE**. In the meantime, Bluster Conjurat, the city's **SHAMAN** (the real one!) announced that he would use *powerful magic* to make our enemies flee. But he was always making **big promises** that he didn't keep, so no one believed him.

At the same time, the village leader, **Ernest Heftymouse**, led the defense

CLACK CLACK

I will do incredible magic!

I'll believe it when I see it!

Umm...

operations. Two mice carried him around the city in a litter made of a **HUGE** tortoise shell.

"Ready the STINKOSAURUSES! Prepare the itching powder! Fill the catapults!"

The **WILD FELINE WARRIORS** charged over our city walls, but our rodent army was ready for them.

First, they used catapults to **HURL** buckets of disgusting brown sludge at the tigers.

"Yuck!" roared the tigers.

Then the balloonosauruses flew overhead, and the cavemice

showered our enemies with **itching powder** made from stinging nettles.

"It itches!" yelled the tigers, scratching themselves furiously.

Finally, the stinkosauruses sprayed the invaders with their *smelly* spray.

"Aaahhh!" screeched the tigers. They turned and **ran** from the city with their tails between their legs. The city's super stinky defense was a success!

VICTORY!

The tigers **FLED** and didn't look back. The rodent army let out a cheer.

"WE WON!"

"We're the strongest!"

"Long live the cavemice!"

I hurried to *The Stone Gazette* to quickly chisel the **NEWS**. When I got to the office, I ran into Thea, who was excited.

"Well done, Geronimo!" she *congratulated* me. "You got the **STONE OF FIRE** back from the tigers!"

"Yes," I replied **happily**. "Hercule and I returned it to the mouseum, where it's on display."

That night, the whole village celebrated with a great banquet of **cheese soup**, Greasella's fried **cheese nuggets**, and roasted meat with **cheese sauce**.

What a great party!

YUM, what a delicious prehistoric feast!

At the end of the meal, the village musicians began to **PLAY** their wooden and stone instruments. Everyone jumped up and **danced** in a line around the table.

It was a wild Stone Age party!

Unfortunately, Chattina Heftymouse, the **wife** of the village leader, sat down next to me. For the rest of the banquet she **TALKED** nonstop.

PREHISTORIC MANNERS

(FOR CAVEMICE ONLY)

At the table, you must:

BURP AT THE END OF THE MEAL.

BLOW YOUR NOSE IN YOUR NAPKIN.

WIPE YOUR DIRTY PAWS ON YOUR NEIGHBOR'S SHIRT.

NOISILY SLURP UP YOUR SOUP.

REMEMBER TO SPIT OUT THE BONES.

"This victory is all thanks to my dear Ernest!" she said proudly. "Then again, it's thanks to me, too. I'm the one who gave him such good *advice*."

A few seats down, Bluster Conjurat, the shaman, stared into his bowl of **cheese** soup. "I see . . . I see . . . that we have won the battle, but not the war," he muttered **GLOOMILY**. "Tiger

Chattina Heftymouse

Khan and his Saber-Toothed Squad will soon return to attack us!"

"Ernest and I agree," said Chattina, holding up a piece of meat as if it were a club. "These **TIGERS** will surely try to steal one of our wonderful inventions again."

"Speaking of **INVENTIONS**," interrupted Fern Fossilfur, the mouseum director, "I have an important announcement to make! Thanks to two brave citizens of our village, the **STONE OF FIRE** has been returned to the mouseum!"

"**oooooooh!**" everyone exclaimed.

"I'd like to thank the two **HEROES** who faced countless dangers to return it to us," she continued. "Hercule and Geronimo!"

Everyone at the banquet burst into cheers and applause.

"LONG LIVE GERONIMO!"

"LONG LIVE HERCULE!"

In the end, it all turned out for the best — at least this time. But here in the **STONE AGE**, life can be as hard as a block of petrified cheddar! I'll be on the lookout for my next **ADVENTURE**, or I'm not

Geronimo Stiltonoot, cavemouse!

WANT TO READ THE NEXT ADVENTURE OF THE CAVEMICE? I CAN'T WAIT TO TELL YOU ALL ABOUT IT!

WATCH YOUR TAIL!

Geronimo Stiltonoot wakes up to a terrible morning. Meteors are falling from the sky, and everyone in Old Mouse City has an awful stomachache! Geronimo must travel to the Cave of Memories to find the ancient shaman cure for his fellow cavemice. But dangers lurk on his journey — can he make it back home safely?

Don't miss any of my other fabumouse adventures!

#1 Lost Treasure of the Emerald Eye

#2 The Curse of the Cheese Pyramid

#3 Cat and Mouse in a Haunted House

#4 I'm Too Fond of My Fur!

#5 Four Mice Deep in the Jungle

#6 Paws Off, Cheddarface!

#7 Red Pizzas for a Blue Count

#8 Attack of the Bandit Cats

#9 A Fabumouse Vacation for Geronimo

#10 All Because of a Cup of Coffee

#11 It's Halloween, You 'Fraidy Mouse!

#12 Merry Christmas, Geronimo!

#13 The Phantom of the Subway

#14 The Temple of the Ruby of Fire

#15 The Mona Mousa Code

#16 A Cheese-Colored Camper

#17 Watch Your Whiskers, Stilton!

#18 Shipwreck on the Pirate Islands

#19 My Name Is Stilton, Geronimo Stilton

#20 Surf's Up, Geronimo!

#21 The Wild, Wild West

#22 The Secret of Cacklefur Castle

A Christmas Tale

#23 Valentine's Day Disaster

#24 Field Trip to Niagara Falls

#25 The Search for Sunken Treasure

#26 The Mummy with No Name

#27 The Christmas Toy Factory

#28 Wedding Crasher

#29 Down and Out Down Under

#30 The Mouse Island Marathon

#31 The Mysterious Cheese Thief

Christmas Catastrophe

#32 Valley of the Giant Skeletons

#33 Geronimo and the Gold Medal Mystery

#34 Geronimo Stilton, Secret Agent

#35 A Very Merry Christmas

#36 Geronimo's Valentine

#37 The Race Across America

#38 A Fabumouse School Adventure

#39 Singing Sensation

#40 The Karate Mouse

#41 Mighty Mount Kilimanjaro

#42 The Peculiar Pumpkin Thief

#43 I'm Not a Supermouse!

#44 The Giant Diamond Robbery

#45 Save the White Whale!

#46 The Haunted Castle

#47 Run for the Hills, Geronimo!

#48 The Mystery in Venice

#49 The Way of the Samurai

#50 This Hotel is Haunted!

#51 The Enormouse Pearl Heist

Don't miss these very special editions!

THE KINGDOM OF FANTASY

THE QUEST FOR PARADISE: THE RETURN TO THE KINGDOM OF FANTASY

THE AMAZING VOYAGE: THE THIRD ADVENTURE IN THE KINGDOM OF FANTASY

THE DRAGON PROPHECY: THE FOURTH ADVENTURE IN THE KINGDOM OF FANTASY

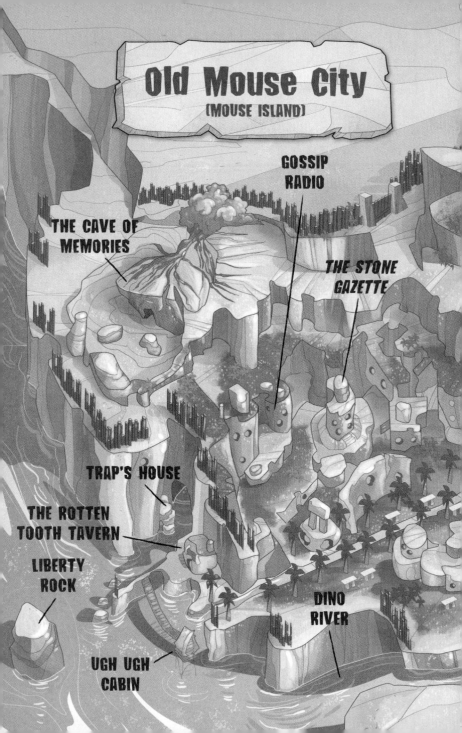

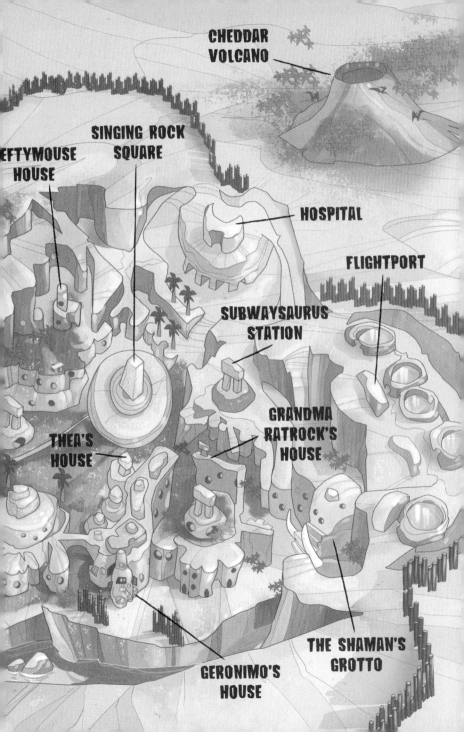

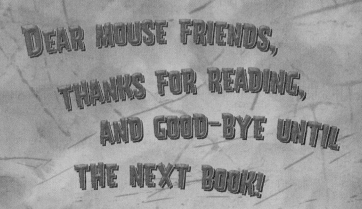

DEAR MOUSE FRIENDS,

THANKS FOR READING,

AND GOOD-BYE UNTIL

THE NEXT BOOK!